TEAM DIVINE D

KNOCK, KNOCK- NUCLEAR THREAT IS HERE

DAIWIK KHARYAL

Made with ♥ on the Notion Press Platform
www.notionpress.com

**Dedicated to all those ignited young minds
of the universe who dare a dream to save
the world and humanity**

Contents

Disclaimer

All the characters, places, scenes, story, pictures of this book are fictional. It is not linked to any person, place, story or scene in reality. Resemblance if any, will be merely a coincidence..

English Version Of A Hindi Science Fiction Book

This book is english language version of hindi language science fiction book

डिवाइन डी - परमाणु खतरे की आहट

written by author, Mr. Daiwik Kharyal

We all might have read about human history. Since the early history of his origin, human race has done many inventions knowingly or unknowingly. These inventions has eased many lives. Science has been just a tool of progression in the human hand yet there are some recorded stances where these inventions has completely overpowered him. Some of the renowned scientists has never thought that their inventions have enough potential to end the life from the universe. When famous Physicist Robert J. Oppenheimer and his team invented hydrogen bomb, they might not have thought even in dreams that their discovery will wreck a havoc at such an extent one day. It had led to complete destruction of two cities of Japan, Hiroshima and Nagasaki. Millions of people lost their life. Science is disasterous if it falls in the hand of wrongdoers. In modern world, many science inventions and discoveries of science has made our life more convenient but what will happen if these experiments are hacked for misfortune. Can we save life on earth ? How can we tackle these threats?

In many TV cartoons, I have watched that in the climax scenes, whenever the lives are in danger on the earth, Superhreroes appear and save them by averting any possible danger. But in reality, will it happen ? Will a superhero really there to save our endangered future? Else do we have to become our superheroes ourselves ? But How ? We don't have superpowers with us. Should I create my own superheroes' team instead of watching these on TV ? Is it Possible ? Is it worthy ? Oh Yes, I should try atleast. Then I thought for a while, picked the pen and wrote something on a paper. In the very next moment, my mind rejected it.

Then I wrapped it, tore it and rewrote it. It is a cycle of art world and rejection is a mandatory part of it. Then I started accepting these rejections. How can I pass on raw thoughts to the readers until I am not able to convince myself ? So many unfinished stories and ideas are still in my unconscious mind just like many untold dreams. After 5-6 months long scheduled cycle of acceptance, rejection and improvements, finally my draft was ready to share with my parents who further undertook responsibility of illustration and editorial part. As promised my mom and dad, they also delivered their commitments and afterall, my first ever hindi literary effort DIVINE D- PARMANU KHATRE KI AAHAT was published by Notion Press Pvt Ltd. Thanks to voice typing tool of our laptop which exempts tidy and hectic work of hindi typing. I am glad to see the overwhelmed response and recognition from hindi readers.

This is how my juvenile literary journey has been kickstarted and I want to carry it further. So I am grabbing this oppurtunity to penetrate into the non-hindi language readers' minds. So, with the strong support of my parents and cousin sister Ms Paavni Jaswal, I have translated hindi version of this book into english language with title **"Team Divine D- Knock, Knock-Nuclear threat is here"**. It is a science fiction story of three common African tribal 10th grade school students and their dog who mysteriously get superpowers and then their aim is to counter the devil powers of the world. Hope you all will read and like my first english language literary attempt.

Daiwik Kharyal

Preface

Daiwik Kharyal

The Divine D Anthem

Divine D, Divine D,
We are team Divine D
We are like flying kites,
always fight for people's right.
Let's together join hand,
let's make a strong stand.
We Are Young and we are brave,
devils cannot make us Slave.
we can sting like a bee,
we are team Divine D.

Born on November 12, 2013 at Aghar village in Hamirpur district of Himachal Pradesh, India, Daiwik Kharyal has started his academic journey From Dhilwan International Public School (DIPS) Suranussi, Jallandhar, Punjab, India. After that his academic wheels rolled through different schools like Mount Maurya International Public School Joginder Nagar, Alpine Public School Nalagarh in Himachal Pradesh stateof India. Currently, he is pursuing his education in the 6th standard at MRA DAV Public School Solan, H.P. Diverse educational environments of these institutons enabled him to think out of the box and deepened his interest in writing and artwork activities. He displayed it recently when he got a chance to sketch a picture in the preface of a hindi poetry book, Baal Prahar which was published earlier this year. The optimistic and persistent encouragement forced him to take this opportunity as a challenge when his skill development teacher assigned him to draft any comic or imaginary story in the class. He drafted a small rough booklet and named it PORAMAN. It was a tiny but sparking moment when he got a positive note from the teacher as well as parents. His parents promised him if he will keep on writing good plots, they will definitely help to get his work published at good platform. Also they promised him to handle the artwork part of his manuscript.

He never looked back and started to write a hindi science fiction story book from that day. It was never easy for a ten year boy, but he chose to write fiction instead of watching TV cartoon for hours. He consulted parents for technical or scientific queries and kept himself riding on horse of imagination. After 5-6 months of regular engagement with daily morning and evening precious hours, his efforts florished as DIVINE D- PARMANU

KHATRE KI AAHAT, his first hindi science fiction book got published by Notion Press India Pvt Ltd. The story was related to three common school students and their uncommon superheroeic acts to counterfoil the attempt of mighy villains to misuse the nuclear powers.

Being called young author by colleagues and readers, Mr. Daiwik Kharyal has now tasted the literary apetizer and kickstarted his juvenile literature journey and committed to reach out non-hindi readers and decided to translate it into english language. With help of his parents and cousin Ms Paavni Jaswal, its english version "Team Divine D- Knock, knock- Nuclear threat is here" in now ready for publication again. Although it is a fiction story, readers can still relate to the real message the author wants to convey in the book. Hope the readers will enjoy reading this literary attempt by very young budding author.

Acknowledgements

First of all, I would like to thank godess Saraswati Maa for blesing bless me with this skill. I would take this opportunity to thank my parents and grandparents whose support is as critical as my back bone's in my life. I would like to thank my school (MRA DAV Public School Solan) Principal, Ms. Masooma Singha ma'am, all my school teachers with special mention of Ms Pooja Sharma ma'am, my class teacher (also my english language teacher) and Ms Natasha ma'am (Skill Development teacher, Ex english language teacher), Amita Sharma, Apoorva Mam (Ex class teachers) who inculcated art of writing and enabled me to think out of the box. I am also thankful to Mr Amar Singh sir, Librarian, MRA DAV Public Schhol Solan for his constant guidance towards creative writing. I received constatnt motivation from my cousins Paavni Jaswal, Devansh Jaswal, Neha Singh, Priyanka Singh, Yamini Singh, Shaiphaly Ranaut, Srijan Ranaut and Divyam Singh. I would like to thank all my friends and relatives for their love and support. At last, Notion Press India Pvt Ltd deserves a special mention without whom this publishing wouldn't have been posssible.

Introduction of Characters

Heroes :- Team Divine D

Duma :- The leader of superheroes team Divine D, an ordinary 14 years old tribal 10th grade student from Malugi village in Sudalu region of Africa continent who transforms as a superhero with divine powers. He establishes Team DIVINE D alongwith his two friends. Brilliant skills and knowledge about science.

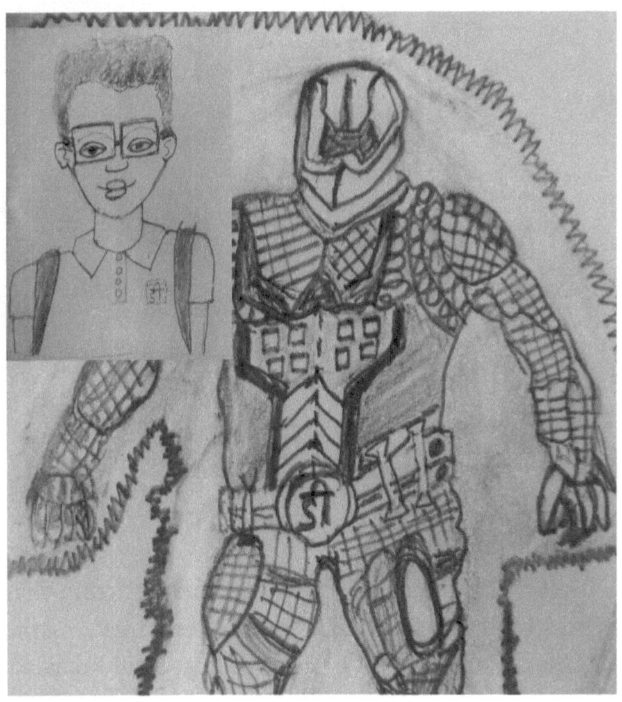

Duma

Damond :- Duma's friend and 2nd member of team DIVINE D. Excellent skills and deep knowledge about weapons and instruments engineering. Fine sketch artist. Can create dummy instruments looking like original ones.

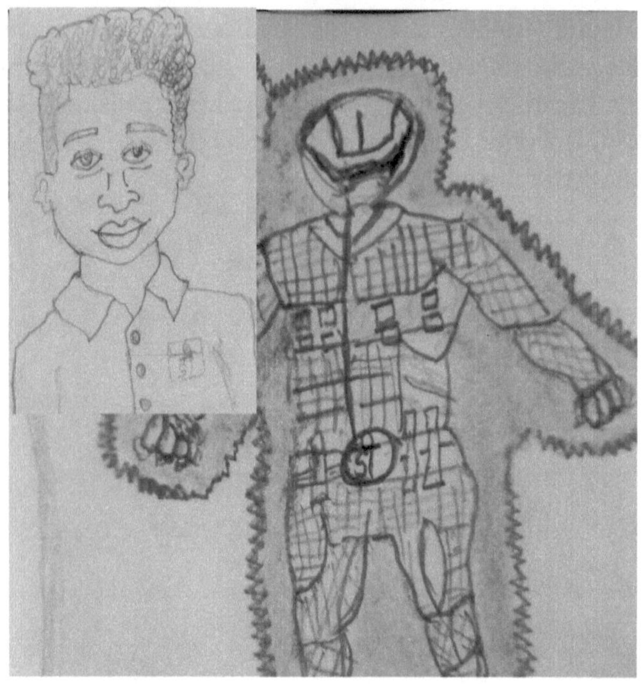

Dasmond

Diara:- Third and only female member of team Divine D, friend of Duma and Dasmond. Extraordinary memory about roads, maps, events etc. genius in general knowledge.

Diara

Dodi :- The fourth and last member of team Divine D, a puppy, excellent sniffing power to smell the things after he got super powers

Dodi

Villains team :- M-4

Mbaka- An infamous ex-nuclear sciientist from Africa, nuclear weapon expert, Aim is to rule the world.

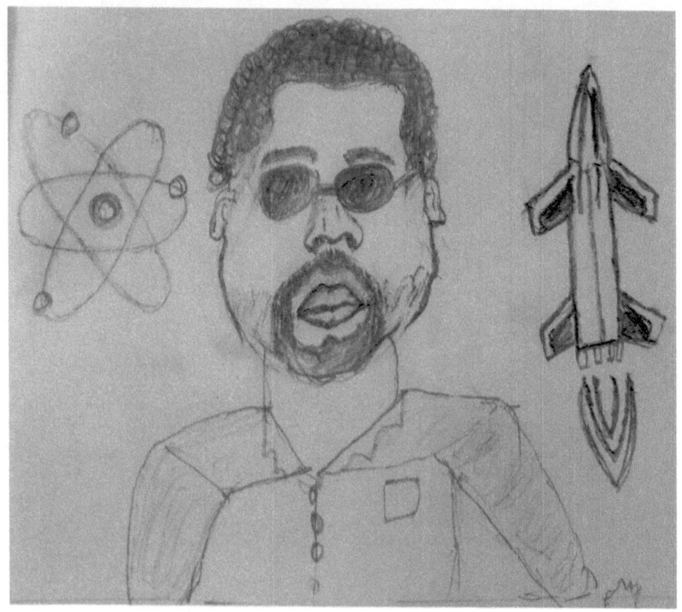

Mr Mbaka

Dr Ming :- A famous researcher biologist from China. Expert for experiment with animals. Aim is to become a master of biologists and create breeds of creatures of his choice. In fact, he wants to control the entire animal kingdom.

Dr Ming

Sargeant Milankova : Third member of M-4. Ex Commondo and Spy from Russia. Expert in breaking any security system. Expert of martial art and can steal information worldwide.

Sargeant Milanikova

Mario De Costa (MDC) :- Popularly known as MDC, a Mexican, infamous financer of dark world. Potential to form and overthrow any political organization

Mario De Costa (MDC)

URANI :- A special mutated dark monkey invented by Dr Ming using combination of DNA technology and nuclear power. Elder brother of demolition. Can emit nuclear rays through mouth and eys, weapon like strong long steel blade claws, night vision, can resize body as per situation, a flexible hidden pouch in the body to collect uranium, ability to jump from building to building. Can cross water channels without fatigue.

Urani

Plutoni :- The younger brother of demolition. Extreme power to bend a bundle of ten thick iron pipes at once. Rest powers are like URANI.

Plutoni

1

The threat of nuclear danger

It was the time when the whole world was experienceing the extreme aftereffects of global warming. situations were beyond imagination. People were dying with floods, draughts, wildfire, famine etc unnaturally. Superpower countries of the world were locking horn with each other to control over nuclear plants and weapons. Governments of aleardy fargile countries were failing as well as falling. Meantime some devil forces were trying to get control over nuclear weapons all over the world. With objective to rule the world, four genius otherwise notorious work professionals, Mr Mbaka, Dr Ming, Sargeant Milanikova and MDC (Mario D'Costa) were working on a very dangerous project " THE DARK MONKEYS" In their lab M-4 Research Centre in a distant moraba Island. Here is their first meeting

M-4

Mr Mbaka:- Hey friends, welcome. Myself Mr Mbaka, a nuclear scientist from Africa, expert in designing nuclear weapons and my ambition is to rule the world.

Dr Ming: Myself Dr Ming, Senior Research Biologist from Zuzong Animal Research Station China. I can transform any animal to bigger and powerful creature and want to make my own animal kingdom with use of genetic techniques.

Milanikova :- Myself Sargeant Milanikova, Ex commando and secret services spy of Russian federation. I can break any security system and steal the sensitive informations.

MDC (Mario D'Costa) :- Myself Mario D'Costa, you can call me MDC, business tycoon of the dark world. I can make and break powers with heap and heat of currency.

I am fine, world is mine.

why you fear, when MDC is here

Mr Mbaka:- Welcome gentlemen, welcome to Moraba Island. Let me tell you that I have settled my umpire here 10 years ago. In my mission to rule the world, I have installed nuclear plants, reactors very secretly here. But that's not enough to control this planet. We need more powers, weapons, advance technologies. That's why I need you all to accompany and achieve the mission.

Dr Ming :- Thanks dear, I am expert in animal research. Why do you need me in this mission.

Mbaka:- Ha ha ha ha, cool down Doctor, I have a master plan for you all. you all are gems of the dark world.

MilaniKova :- What's our profit in it ?

Mbaka:- Oh dear, oh dear, only profit will not define our success. Very sooon, we will be rulers of this universe. It is an endless game.

MDC:- Mr Mbaka , who will lead the mission ?

Mbaka :- It is open for all of us, we all are pioneer leaders of our own fields. You can suggest, how can we choose a single leader?

Dr Ming:- That's not a big issue, you are the plan master, I have no objection to notimate you as head of the mission.

Milanikova & MDC:- We too.

Mbaka:- Thanks guys, let's celebrate the foundation day of M-4.

Dr Ming :- What's the plan ahead Boss Mbaka ?

Mbaka :- MISSION DARK MONKY is the first project of M-4.

Dr Ming :- Dark Monkey ! Quite strange and interesting title. Will monkeys have something to do or just a code name ?

Mbaka :- Yes, yes doctor, Monkeys will be our soldiers in this mission. We will transform common monkeys into our specially trained dark monkeys' army with use of nuclear energy and your genetical Supremacy . They will search more uranium for us.

MDC :- What monkeys have to do with Uranium ?

Mbaka :- Monkey have nothing to do but we have to. Monkeys are just carrriers.

Milanikova :- How ?

Mbaka :- Uranium is life line of our project. We need nuclear energy for our nuclear programs, nuclear weapons and ultimately to rules the world..

MDC :- How is Uranium formed.

Mbaka :- Uranium was probably formed in supernova events billions of years ago. It is a heavy metal and a explosive source of energy.

Milanikova :- Why monkeys only and how dark monkeys army will work ?

Mbaka :- That's exactly a master plan. Monkeys have many characteristic similaritis with human beings. If mutated and prperly trained, they will easily scan and search the source of Uranium and can dig and bring it for us. , Dr Ming will handle the genetic mutation part and training part you will have to take care.

Dr Ming :- It's quite interesting and with in my scope. I'm sure something can be done. Let's fix it.

Mbaka :- Once Dr. Ming's work is over, I will check for nuclear mutation part. Then they will be handed over to you for inculcating commandos skills and spy techniques.

Milanikova :- That's great. From where, we can get the uranium sources ?

Mbaka :- Australia, Canada, Russia, Kazakhstan and in many more places of the world. But this time we will target my homeland, Sudalu region in Africa.

MDC :- Why Sudalu region ?

Mbaka :- A lot of reasons, but the mainly due to security situations, laws and resemblance of monkey species between here and Sudalu region.

Dr Ming :- I can understand little bit. Mainland Africa is not far away from us. our mutated monkeys will easily mix up with their common monkeys and do the work.. What About the security ?

Milanikova :- Leave it to me. I have been in secret services in Nigeria, Congo, Burundi and other African countries. Security situations are not very tight there. We can exploit that.

Mbaka :- Oh that's great. It will work. There are many rebels and terrorist groups in some hunger driven areas. We can offer some money and weapons and they may work for us. But we will never reveal our plan to these people.

MDC :- Wonderful. I can invested in it. Any more detail ?

Mbaka :- Sudalu state is the least developed region of Africa. people are waiting to dethrow the dictator, General Mussaba. During my stay at nuclear Research Station Sendora, We had research finding that there are uranium ores there in the rocks of Sudalu region. We will overturn the General Mussaba's forces with help of this rebels and will take food control of Sudalu.

Milaniova :- A lot of unrest and unemployment there. It's a golden chance with less risk for us.

Mbaka :- We have captured some monkeys from that region and are kept in our lab. Let's start with them. Boom Boom.

2

Team Divine D :- The young warriors of Sudalu

Team Divine D

In Malugi region of Africa, an underprivilege school boy called Duma was living with his family, a hunter gatherer cum tailor father, a housewife mother and three siblings. He is slim, frazile and physically weak student of the 10th stardard. So classmates were often making fun of his physical appearance. He was very intelligent in academics and brilliant student of the class specially in science subject. Despite of that, he had not made many friends except Diara and Dasmond as he was very shy. One day, while coming back from school, they found a poor little puppy who started walking beside them. Duma loved that puppy and decided to carry it to his home.

Duma :- Hey lovely puppy! how cute you are. I want to take you to my home, but my mom doesn't like pets. Don't worry, I will still keep you safe and hidden there.

Diara (Girl) :- Hey Duma! Where will you keep it ?

Duma :- Don't know exactly, but can't let him wandering here and there.

Dasmond :- Hey ! I have an idea, if you like it.

Duma :- Oh yes, tell me.

Dasmond :- We can keep him in our Mini lab, THE DIVINE D PLANET .

Duma :- That's good idea, But what about his meal? Our families are too poor to provide food to us. How can they afford bread for this puppy?

Diara :- And this puppy may destroy our mini world THE DIVINE D PLANET, toy inventions.

Duma :- We can provide a separate space for him there and in the day time it may accompany us and sit outside school.

Dasmond :- And food ?

Duma:- See Dasmond and Diara, for food, we can plead to our parents. We have to spare some food from our lunch boxes. Are you ok with it ?

Dasmond :- Hmm for the sake of his life, I can.

Diara :- Me too. What should be its name ?

Dasmond :- It sould start with letter D as he is new member of The Divine D team

Duma :- Let it be Dodi ?

Diara :- Dodi means ?

Duma :- Gift or well loved.

Dasmond :- That's sond nice. Let it. Welcome Dodi to the D team.

3

The Divine D Planet

The time rolled and team Divine D was now more happy after inclusion of Dodi, the puppy in their team. Dodi accompanied other members of team Divine D to the school and back to their bamboo hut mini lab THE DIVINE D PLANET.

The Divine D Planet

Some school boy are bullying members of team Divine D

Boy 1 :- Hey boys, look at the poor puppy of Duma, it seems like a mouse. may be younger brother of Duma.

Second boy :- Ha ha Ha ha........

Duma:- Hey ! leave my puppy alone. He is not a mouse. His name is Dodi.

Diara :- Dodi mens gift.

Third boy: - ha ha, It is not a gift, it is a curse, poor choice.

Dasmond :- Don't judge a book from its cover.

Boy 1 :- It is only cover, no book inside. ha ha Ha ha.

Duma :-Don't make fun, one day he will be transformed into a super dog.

All three Boys :- Ha ha, What a joke, keep joking, you Jokers. Let's go. We will visit again for your new laughing stock. you are a good joker.

Duma :- Ok no problem, today we are weak, poor. You can laugh on us. Surely a day will come when we will become more stronger and save the world.

Boy 1 :- Oh really ? We will wait for that day, Duma & Company. Bye for now.

Duma, Dasmoond, Diara and Dodi, all were physically weak, but they had some God gifted talents. Duma was brilliant in science & experimentation. Diara had extraordinary general knowledge of the world. She also had superstrong memory. Dasmond was excellent in art and mechanical skills. He had made real sketches of Isaac Newton, Albert Einstein, Stephen Hawkins etc. They constructed a bamboo hut for their skill showcasing and named it THE DIVINE D PLANET. There were a lot of concept toys vehicle, dresses of imaginary Superheroes.They had made them from scrap & waste materials. One day their science teacher, Mr Miraka visited this mini lab & was very impressed with the Divine D team. He advised them to prepare a science project on a theme 'Just Imagine' on the occasion of International Science Day.

Miraka:- Hey guys, your concepts are miraculous. I think after graduating from the school, you should try in greater institutes of sciences in USA or other advanced countries. One day you will make proud not only Sudalu, but whole Africa.

Duma :- Thank you sir, but we all are so poor that our family can't afford higher studies for us. Studying in USA is next to impossible dream for us. But still we will try.

Miraka:- Don't worry. I have seen your scientific skills and capabilities. I have seen your vision. You will definitely serve the humanity. I will help you all as I can. You just try.

Diara :- Wow! that's great sir. Definitely we will work hard and make you proud.

Miraka :- You prepare a concept project for International Science Day exhibition on theme '**Just Imagine**'. You tell me whatever raw material you need for the project. I will provide you.

Dasmond :- Thank you very much sir. we will start from today itself.

Miraka :- My querry is that after whole day spent in the school, how do you manage time for such activities.

Duma:- Sir, in the evening after doing school homework and household works, we all gather here and do such work for 2 to 3 hours daily. Sometime we skip our meal to get our target completed. We all have great fun in doing this.

Miraka :- That's incredible. All the best guys, do your work. I will always be there whenever you need me.

All three :- Thanks sir.

They started working on it and after some days they built three Divine D Suits which can absorb the nuclear rays in case of nuclear radiation failure or weapon attack. This suit had an instrument installed in it which converts nuclear radiation into muscle power. The theme was to save the human beings from negative impact of nuclear radiations and to generate muscle power.

4

Just Imagine

Miraka: - Students, welcome to JUST IMAGNE. Now you can showcase your future concepts.

Jilusu :- Sir, I have made a supercar. Its speed is 1500Km/hr. The concept is that it will save a lot of time of travelers

Koyala :- Sir I have made a robots who can do all household functions like dish washing, clothes cleaning. Concept behind is that it will reduce a lot of labour burden from my mother's shoulders. She has no time to rest.

Miraka : And Duma you ?

Duma :- Sir me, Diara and Dasmond collectively made four super suits THE DIVINE D SUITS, nuclear radiations absorbing dresses. Two of them are for males, one for females and last one is for animals. The concept behind it is that in case of any nuclear power failure or nuclear weapon attack, it will absorb the nuclear radiations and convert it into muscle power. More the radiation outbreak, more muscle power will be generated instaed of hazard.

Divine D Dress

Principal:- Quite innovatiive! but looking not so practically viable, why we need such suits for this region of Africa where there no nuclear plant estabishment nearby us, hence no such threats. Why people of Africa need it? Can you explain Mr Duma?

Duma :- Sir, With advancing mode of transportation, whole world is now just reduced to a globe. Africa has potential for many raw materials. Developed nations have an eye on us. The day is not far away when some devil forces may attack us. Exploitation is everywhere in Africa now.

Principal :- Oh, Thats the point. Ok, anyway thanks for such brilliant Idea.

That whole day was vibrant with young mind's tidal energy. After so many ideas, concepts and concerns, the selection panel reached out at a consensus and conclusion and the the team Divine D to be awarded with the first prize of 100 USD for Divine D suit cocept. They also decided to send their concept for next level exhibition. The team Divine D was overjoyed. The 100 USD was huge blessing for them & they decided to spend it wisely. Little amount was spent for celebration and rest was kept for the renovation of THE DIVINE D PLANET.

5

The Two Brothers of Demolition

Today on the first anniversary of M-4 lab, all four members are holding a special meeting

Mbaka :- Friends, welcome on special occasion of M-4. Today we are here togather for progress report of our Misson, THE DARK MONKEY. Can we start with you Dr Ming ?

Dr Ming :-Yes Thanks Mr Mbaka. My work is over now. I have introgressed the required traits in the two monkey bosses. Equipped them with Super strong digging mtallic blade like nails and ability to resize them. Hopefully they will deliver their best.

Mbaka :- Great. Alongside Dr Ming, I have also incorporated radiations power in them. Now no common living creature can overpowers them. For training part, over to you Sargeant Milanikova.

Sargeant Milanikova :- To see My Training Part You have to go to lab cage where both our supernovas are being kept.

Mbaka :- Lets move
(IN LAB CAGE)

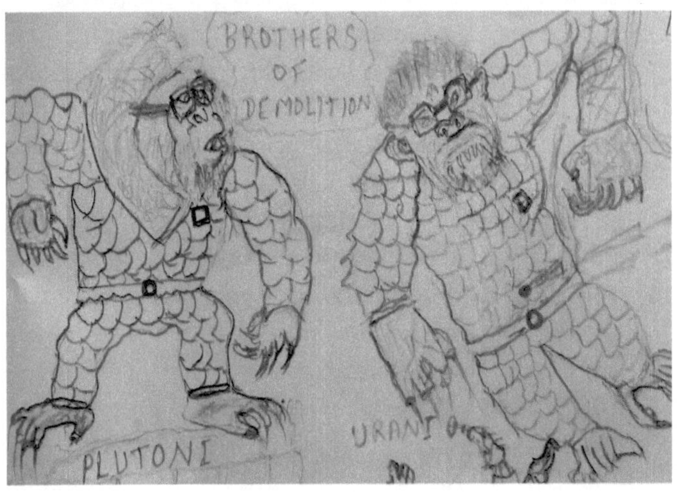

Bothers of demolition

Milanikova :- See our two Supernovas URANI and PLUTONI, the brothers of demolition. They are trained in martial arts and gorilla war. Spy cam & chip is fixed in their body to scan the area with digital powers system which is also linked to our computer system.

Dr Ming :- I have introgressed human vocal traits in them and now they can speak and understand human languages. Let Urani introduced himself. Urani, Can you speak.

Urani :- Hi Boss, I am Urani, elder brother of demolition. Unlike other monkeys, I can see at night, change my body size according to situation. I have such sharp sickles like metallic nails that I can dig the rock and soil very quickly. I can emit nuclear radiations from my eyes as well as hands and finish the target in few seconds.

Mbaka: Now Plutoni, you tell.

Plutoni :- Myself Plutoni, younger brother of demolition. I can Swim very fast, can hold my breath in water for long. I can bend strong 10 iron poles alltogether. Like brother Urani, I can dig, have hidden pouch to collect uranium, change my size and have night vision. I can jump from building to building very quickly.

Mbaka :- They have sensors to detect the uranium ores in soil. They will detect uranium ores, collect and return to us. Then we will do the research on it and we we will overpower the whole region with help of dark monkey army and control all the uranium land.

MDC :- Thats wonderful idea. Who will drop them to Sudalu.

Milanikova :- No need. They are excellent swimmer. They have trained to swim past water bays, rivers, oceans, canals and channels. They will reach at their target in Sudalu region and start excavation work. At first they will get mixed with local monkeys at daytime and at night, they will start their scanning & excavation work as they have night vision trait.

MDC :- Any weakness ?

Dr Ming :- Their long time memory is one of the major concern. After spending long time away from us, they may not differentiate between their bosses and enemies. They have to return within particular period of time.

Mbaka :- Can be fiix it ?

Dr Ming :- Yes we can, but it may take a very long period

Milanikova :- As this mission is of short duration, we can send them now & can take calculated risk. After their returning, we can proceed with their upgradations. We will have their other communication control.

Mbaka :- How long their memory will last ?

Dr Ming :- One month. Although I have placed a memory chip beneath their ears. It will work for five more months. But since it is external, it will work unitil any external force touches or damages it.

Mbaka :- Thats good. Who will dare to touch them ? They are Demon. They will tore apart their opponents in few seconds.

MDC :- You are right Mr Mbaka. We can Proceed with our first mission THE DARK MONKEY.

Mbaka:- With permission of you all, can we start it tomorrow ?

All three :- Sure. lets rock. Hip Hip Hurray.

6

Threat to nuclear scientists' life

International Atomic Energy Centre (IAEC) H.Q., Pricasa

International Atomic Energy Research Centre

Dr Michael Regal :- Welcome to the IAERC Annual Meeting, Hope you are all doing good.

Dr Penn :- Thanks Dr Michael, Our nuclear programs are doing good. but major threat is security concerns.

Dr Russell :- Since last 3 years, our four senior nuclear scientists are either missing or dead mysteriously.

Dr Padmarajan :- We are getting unknown threats. Government has to be very serious for our Safety.

Dr Santiago :- And we are not able to find out who are culprits. It's a serious issue.

Dr Feng Shi : - Since last 10 years a renowned nuclear scientist Dr Mbaka Is missing along with very sensitive material & information. We could not locate his whereabout. Now it's worrying thing for all of us.

Dr Michael Regal :- Gentleman I can understand your point. In the last year meeting also, I have raised questions to many governments regarding this. I will do once again. Any other point ?

Dr Padmarajan :- Sir some countries are not transparent regarding their nuclear programs. they are not sharing their data. What can be done now ?

Dr Michael Regal :- We should be very much concerned on this topic. Geopolitics may unstable our nuclear programs. It may be quite problematic. We are in regular touch with other international organisations. Hope to find out solution very soon.

Dr Penn :- Sir, there are some rumours that inside some remote unhabitated Islands, Some mysterious activities are going on. Some nuclear programs attempt are in progress illegally. What to say ?

Dr Michael Regal :- Yes I have also heard, but we can't go just after rumours. Intelligence agencies will do their work. But we have to be very careful in near future. Some threats are coming for nuclear weapons and safety of nuclear scientists. We have to take care. Thank you all for coming.

Dr Russell :- Thank you sir, one more point I would like to add that we have to think about safety of our nuclear plants all over the world. that's very very important. Thank you and bye.

7

Inspection of Divine D Devices

The team Divine D (while coming back from school)

Duma:- Hey guys! today evening, we will meet in The Divine D Planet and will work on more refinement concepts of The DIVINE D suits and other devices. We have some money and can purchase some scientific instruments from city mechanical centre and will make these suits more appealing before district level exhibition in science fair there.

Dasmond :- Yes, ofcourse we can. Tomorrow is our school holiday. My cousin will be going to city centre in his vehicle. We can go along with him and purchase the needful materials.

Duma:- Thats great. lets finalize our requirements today by today and we will purchase them tomorrow.

Diara:- Okk, Lets do it. I will take care of Dodi and some repairwork in the hut.

Duma:- It's fine. Lets meet there in the evening.

(Evening 6:00 PM at Divine D Planet Lab)

Duma:- Diara kindly hand over me that diary The Brain of Divine D.

Diara :- Ok. What are you doing with it.

Duma :- There are many concepts, procedures, designs, informations related to the the devices we made and under progress already written in this diary. We will fix what else improvement is still needed in these devices and suits. All suggestions are coded in this diary. We have to fit some more microdevices in the Divine D suits.

Dasmond :- Okk. look these are sketches of these suits. Suggest what more can be done.

Duma :- Ok let me explain. No part of the body can be left exposed. Whatever is exposed, we have to cover that portion with these Divine D Gloves and Divine D shoes.

Diara :- Excellent, But what is speciality of these gloves and shoes.

Duma :- These Divine gloves are not ordinary, They are actually secret weapons covering our hands. The magnetic power of these will help us to stick and anchor with any iron object. These small anchors will help us to climb on a wall, building, rock or tree.

Dasmond :- Wonderful. What about this Divine Super gun ?

Duma :- It is also called control rod gun. It will fire control rods chain which can slow down the speed of neutrons and will stop the nuclaer reaction.

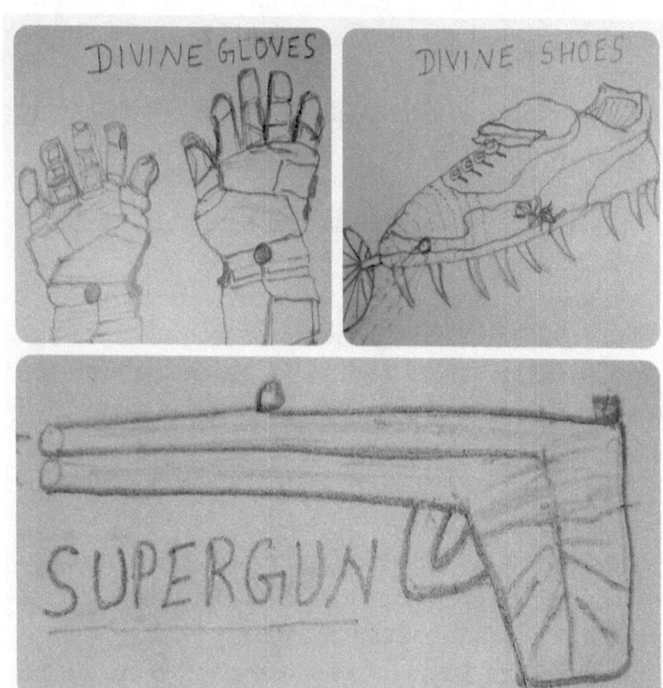

Dvine D Devices

Diara:- Bravo! Control rods are made up of which material ?

Duma :- Boron or Cadmium. Apart from it we will also work on neutron capture technique in near future.

Dasmond :- Now explain working of Divine shoes.

Duma :- They are actually supper flyers. Depending upon the situation, these can decrease or increase our body weight. They can make it even zero. We can fly in air, walk on water or climb the rock easily.

Dasmond :- One suggestion I want to add. The colour of Divine D suits, shoes and gloves should be identical. Will it work?

Duma :- Sure we can. Already these all have camouflage powers, means these can acquire the colour of any background if needed.

Diara :- Master class it is. Now lets start our further work.

Duma :- Yes, my concern is that this diary THE BRAIN OF DIVINE D is mandatory for us all the time, but its size is big, so we can't carry it with us all the time conveniently. We have to reduce its size and make it technology friendly. It may also be torn or lost.

Diara :- It is storehouse or symbol of our capability . We can't afford to lose it.

Dasmond :- We have handsome amount of money still left with us. We can search any electronic gazette from the city centre and pour the content in it.

Duma :- Yes Dasmond, you have a valid point. Any second hand digital watch or note pad can serve our purpose. Recorded content can be saved for long time.

Dasmond :- A junk dealer in the city is well known to my cousin. We will go with him, search our requirements and can bargain.

Duma:- Thats good. Now lets finish today's task. Dodi is also hungry. Lets feed him as well.

After swimming Loko canal for whole day, now both brothers of demolition reached in Sudalu forests, started searching and scanning their target land. This forest was hardly 3 KM far from Malugi village, the village of Team Divine D and very near to their lab THE DIVINE D PLANET. So there were full chances that confrontation between both teams may happen. meanwhile, M-4 Lab again established communication with them.

Dr Ming :- Mr Urani, can you hear me ?

Urani :- Yes boss, I can hear you.

Dr Ming :- Are you in Sudalu forest now ?

Urani :-Yes boss, near our target.

Dr Ming :- Listen, stay there for tonight. Tomorrow morning try to mix with local monkey troops. But beware, they will not allow you join them immediately. You will have to keep patience and try again and again. In the night time do your assigned work.

Urani :- Yes boss we will do the same.

Dr Ming :- Let me remind you, don't do any activity in the daytime. Don't push youselfves under people's scanner.

Plutoni :- Ok Boss

Dr Ming :- Then ok bye. Over and out.

The things happened as usual Ffor 2-3 days. Troops of local mokeys did not entertained these duo. But slowly they gained the trust and confidence of local troops. By some tricks and luring them, they joined the troop. After spending daytime with fellow monkeys, they started searching overnight for uranium ore sources in the forest. Whatever they received, they gathered it in their hidden body pouch. The time had flown and one month was over.

On the other side, the Divine D team has also done their refinement work on the Divine D suits. They installed some advance devices and now these were looking very shiny and attractive. The team was now ready for the next level.

8

The two supernovas of demolition

Everything was going as per plan of M-4 until a blunder surfaced the whole plot. Suddenly laptop of Dr Ming stopped working and all communication control with Urani and Plutoni lost. Both were receiving no routine instructions and commands. It was already one month over and their memory started fading slowly. They were behaving arbitrary. Dr Ming fixed the error and rectify and again tried to regain communication control, but now it was too late. After the clash with fellow moneys, the chips behind their ears got dettached and dropped somewhere. After this revelation, there was a chilling sensation in the M-4 lab.

(M-4 Lab)

Dr Ming :- Friends, I have a bad news for us.

Mr Mbaka :- What happened Dr ? Any communication connection established with supernova team of demolition ?

Dr Ming :- Yes their signls are now intercepted and loction traced but unfortunately they are not responding to us. In fact they are no more in our control.

Mr Mbaka :- Oh ! thats terrible. What if they were arrested or captured by local administration?

Dr Ming :- Its almost next to impossible to control and capture them alive but more worry is that now they are totally autonomous and can wreck a havoc in the city. Before their limelight, we have to trace and either either control or finish them.

Milanikova :- Is it possible ?

Dr Ming :- Yes we can do, but for doing that we have to be within 100 metres radius around their location. Still we have this remote which can control or fuse microtransmitter installed in their chest.

MDC :- That good but think wisely, first we should try to control them alive as there is already huge investment of time and money on them. Destroying them should be our last alternate.

Mr Mbaka : Yes you are right, but no outsider should have the clue and access of our mission. That will be even worse. Let us try for 2-3 days to regain their control otherwise go for last option.

Dr Ming :- But who will go there ?

Milanikova :- Don't worry Dr Ming, I will take the lead and go there in person.

Mr Mbaka :- Thats great Sargeant, You are a real warrior. Lets focus on the assignment.

9

The havoc in Sudalu

As soon as the communication link broken between M-4 and brothers of demolition, they became totally autonomous and started behaving unruly. They started fighting with fellow mokeys in a ruthless manner and scolded them. The monkey troop couldn't handle those mightly demon and fled from there. Forest turned into battleground. Whosoever tried to confront them, might dark monkeys did not space anyone and attacked mercilessly.

Unaware from this hue and cry, few km away, the team Divine D was busy in their final rehearsal for upcoming science sxhibition. They don't want any shortcoming in showcasing their project Divine D suits, So they decided to go for final dress rehearsal before heading towards homes. Today dodi was also part of it.

Duma :- Come on friends, let's wear our Divine dresses and be the superheroes.

Dasmond :- Let's Do

Diara :- Okk lets wear and then also make Dodi the Superdog

Duma :- Ha Ha Ha, you mean Divine Dog

Diara :- Exactly.

(Soon after wearing Divine D Suits)

Duma :- Just Wow, we are looking like superheroes exactly.

Dasmnd :- You are right, best fit.

Diara:- I wish I could wear it daily even in school.

Duma :- Hahaha, may miracle will happen and we will emerge as superheroes.

(Suddenly Dodi started barking at them seeing in new costume)

Diara :- Hey Dodi ! stop, we are superheroes. In a few minutes you will also be a super dog, just cool down.

For sometime they inspected all other instruments in mini lab and after that they dressd up Dodi as well. They were about to leave for homes but none was willing to undress this supercool dress.

Duma :- Her dear, Lets go to home in this new dress. That will be a surprise for our parents. Tomorrow we will display these. Lets display and explain while wearing it on our bodies in the exhibition.

Diara :- Ya, That will be even more appealing. Now lets go home, mom will be very angry. We are already late.

Before they step out for home, Dodi suddenly sensed something and started barking loudly. He ran away towards forest.

Duma :- Hey hey Dodi ! What are you doing? Don't go anywhere. We are leaving for home. Stay here.

But he did not listened to his boss and barked uninterruptly.

Dasmond :- Hey look at the forest. A bright light shining at night, it's unusual. I can hear some screaming voices of animals.

Duma :- Dodi went there already. Lets go and watch.

Diara :- Are you people getting out of mind. Its jungle and now night also. What the hell are you doing ?

Duma :- Dodi has already left for jungle. I can't leave him alone. I have to go. Diara you can stay here or proceed to village. Dasmond are you coming with me ?

Dasmond :- Let's go.

Diara :- Stop, I am also coming.

(When they reached near forest entry point, they can't believe on their eyes. Two giant dark monkeys were on fire. They were roaring instead of chattering and all other wild animals were ruuning here and there)

Diara :- Oh my God! Monster creatures, let's run guys.

Duma :- They are approaching us. They might have seen us. Let's go.

Dasmond :- Dodi, run faster

(After a sprint of few minutes they reached at lab hut)

Diara (overbreathing) :- I am tired, can't run anymore.

Duma :- Are you mad, they are chasing us. In few moments they will be here.

Dasmond :- Trust me, we must hide ourselves inside lab cottage. We can't match their sprint pace.

(Suddenly they all entered inside alongwith Dodi and locked the room)

Duma :- What a brightening and frightening creature are they! I have never seen such animals in my whole life. Horrible look. Very vigorous

Dasmond :- They are looking like half machines. Are they monsters ?

Diara :- No idea, but they are dreaded. I have never heard/read about such creature in any book.

Duma :- How will we compete with those ?

Dasmnd :- Forget about fighting or competing, we can't even stand for few minutes infront of them. They have some amazing power of lightening they were emitting from their hand, eyes and mouth. Thay are roasting everything.

Duma :- We should think like warriors. We can't surrender without fight. We have petrol guns. Whatever may be the end, we will attack them with petrol fireballs.

Dasmnd :- You are right. Now encounter is inevitable. Let's fight with full courage. We are team Divine D. We will fight with our zeal

Diara :- Let's play Divine D anthem

All started singing

Divine D, Divine D,

We are team Divine D

We are like flying kites,

always fight for people's right.

Let's together join hand,

let's make a strong stand

We Are Young and we are brave

devils cannot make us Slave

we can sting like a bee,

we are team Divine D

Now the Divine D team was atleast ready for a face off with mighty brothers of demolition.

10

Divine D - The rise of young superheroes

After roasting wildlife of forest, now Urani and Plutoni were marching towards Malugi village. The whole jungle was screaming. Infuriated Duo started using their nuclear power. Entire surrounding witnessed thunder and lightening of monster power. People of Malugi were also rushing towards site.

Duma :- Take your position guys they are coming.

Dasmond :- we will go out as an unit

Diara :- Ya even if death is inevitable, we will die as superheroes

Duma :- Three, two, one, lets go

(Now both parties were in a face off mode)

Duma :- Hey monsters ! Go back, you can't destroy our native place. This land belongs only to us.

Urani :- You young chicks can't stop us. The place we enter belongs to us only. Run away or get ready to face the consequences.

Duma :- You can't kill innocent animals here. We wouldn't let it happen.

Plutoni :- Won't let it happen ? What can you do?

Diara :- You don't know how powerful are we ?

Plutoni :- Oh really ! my little chicks ? We will rule the world. None can stop us. You just get out from here.

Duma (while loading the petrol bomb in gun):- Then accept our regard for you.

Duma fired the gun and the first fireball hit the shoulder of Urani. This made Urani more irritated and furious.

Urani :- How dare you little rat? Now see my dare now.

Suddenly Dasmond and Diara also tried to grab him and Dodi tried to bite from backside. But red faced both Urani and plutoni threw all of them toward hut. Dodi also got scared and hid himself inside hut.

Urani :- Enough is enough, Plutoni, let's finish their game.

Face off- Power Verses Enthusiasm

Then they suddenly used their nuclear power attack. There was very bright luminous shining & lightening all around. Team Divine D felt a contrast light in front of their eyes and next moment they were unable to see anything around as if they were blind. After approx 15 minute later when they felt some sensation in their bodies again, could not believe on their eyes. Everything had been transformed now. There were unbelievable changes in their bodies. Strong muscular body, tall stature, and moveover a powerhouse of energy. Even their toy devices are looking real one now, What had happened, was beyond imagination. Was it supernatural, magical or Scientific serendipity ? or a never ending speculation how it happened. But It had happened, that was only reality.

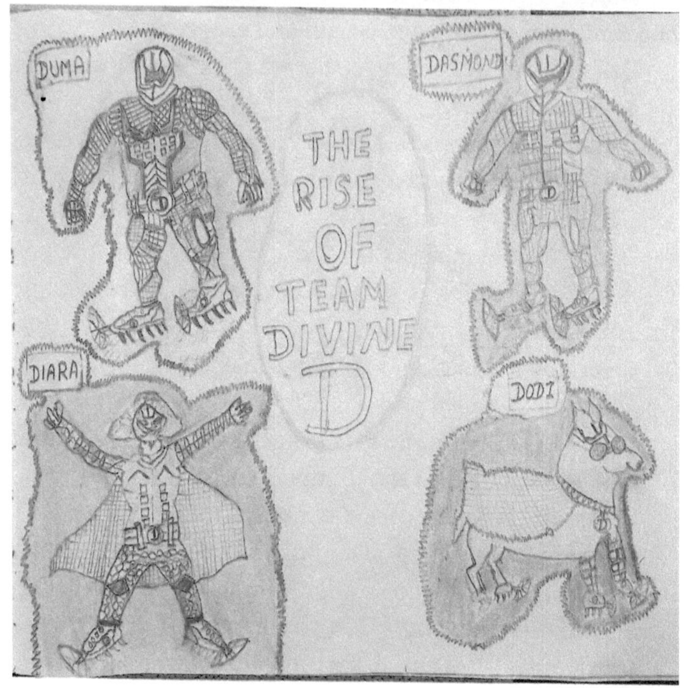

The rise of team Divine D

Before recovering from one shock, another shock was waiting for them when they heard Dodi was speaking in human language.

Dodi :- Hey Duma! get up. They are gone now and destroyed everything here. Let's follow them.

Duma (in disbelief) :- Whats going on, What happened and how are you speaking our language despite being a dog?

Dodi :- Don't know. They have attacked on us with any lightening and thunderous weapon and I contracted an electric shock and fainted.

Diara :- Are we still in a dream or hallucination ? How suddenly we became so powerful and energetic ?

Dasmond :- Lucky thing is that we are still alive and okk. Its new world for us.

Duma :- Our dress is also so shiny. It looks like never before. Realistic, perfectly original and much more appealing than we created.

Diara :- It's looking as original as superheroes dresses. Guys, my gut feeling is that It's devices are activated and transformed to original ones.

Dasmond :- If so, then it's powers may also be real. Is our imagination is turned out to reality ?

Duma :- If so and its powers are activated, we, the wearer of these suits should be called superheroes. Is n't so ?

Diara :- If this is the case, we must check its powers.

Duma :- It may be a joke, but if Dodi can speak and learn humal language, any other miracle or science fiction transformation to reality can also happen. Let's check.

Dasmond :- Why not, unfortunately they destroyed our lab, but our all devices and experimental materials are safe. This is also a miracle.

First of all, Duma pressed the antigravity button of suit and suddenly his body was lifed for few metres like rocket speed. Nervously, he also pressed gravity button and fell down on the floor.

Diara : Oh my God, one moore miracle, miracles happening now. Really can't believe it.

Duma :- Now I can relate the whole episode. There was a minor nuclear power attack from their side on us. It's nuclear power which may be empowering our suits and all other devices. That's secret of our energy now.

Dasmond :- But all these are scrap items. How nuclear energy can activate these without following any standard protocol? I means it's just high serendipity.

Duma :- Science, nature or miracle, I am not sure at all, It has happened in reality thats enough for us. Now let's also check D-Brain watch, the digital version of the brain of Divine D. Will it work? We have recorded all the informations and procedures in it. Lets check it's speaker.

After pressing the ON button of D brain

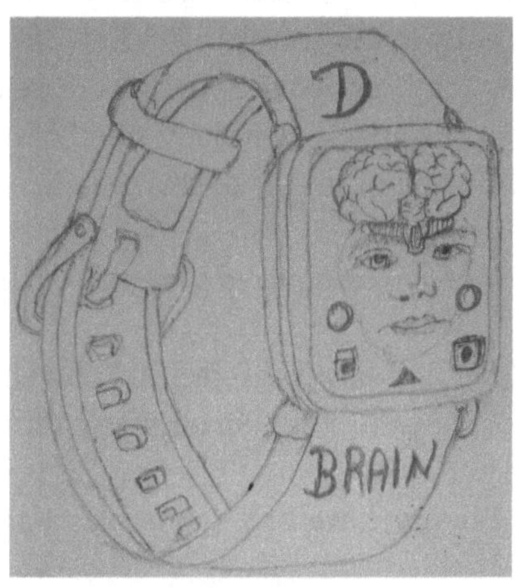

D-Brain

Hello D-Brain, can you help me

D Brain :- Hello Master, what can I do for you ?

Duma (exclaimed with joy) :- Can you explain what happened here few minutes ago ?

D Brain :- Master, two mighty Dark monkey like giant creatures were demolishing everything and your all were lying fainted on ground.

Duma :- D Brain, can you let us know which weapons they used to attack us? I mean which material they used?

D Brain :- Sorry master, I was not activated that time. But still I can tell that there was extreme high temperature and brightness all around. It was so hot that all materials were flamed to ashes in the fire. It was miniature of a powerful nuclear attack. AS per my information, exactally similar attack, but of much higher magnitude might have happened at Hiroshima and Nagasaki cities of Japan during World War-II. They might have used very small amount of Uranium recently in this attack.

Dodi:- My sniffing power has increased manyfold suddenly after the attack. Definitely smell of uranium like element is diffusing in the air of this area now. Let's check the source.

Duma :- Have you recognized the smell of Uranium ever ?

Dodi :- Never, but now I can feel it. It may be due to the mask of my supersuit. I can smell many different smells now.

Duma :- Do you have any guess about their current whereabout ?

D Brain :- Not exactly, as they are beyond my range now. But they have fled towards city.

Duma :- Oh my God! they can cause destruction in the city. We have to trace them as soon as soon possible.

Dasmond :- We should first know how they attacked us and for that we should follow Dodi's footsteps to recent battleground to find uranium sources ?

Diara :- Shouldn't we head towards our village and our parents to alert first ? They might have worried for us by now.

Duma :- Then it will be too late to stop them, D Brain, can you trace whether they went towards Malugi village ?

D Brain :- As per my GPS data, they did not followed a path to Malugi, they directly went to city road. Malugi village is safe.

Duma :- Thanks for update. Friends, we are superheroes and to save all people is our mandate. So let's follow Dodi and locate the source of the powerful metal in our adjoining hill.

All three :- Let's move

11

The review of Divine D powers

When they reached adjoining hill, they shocked to watch the scene there. There was a deep trench in the middle of steep slope of hills

Duma :- Its not possible for any common living being to dig such a big and deep trench without help of advance machinery and even machines can't be taken to such a sloppy hill. How it might have happened ?

Diara :- Other question is that what is the need to dig such a big trench here ?

Dasmond :- Let's reach there and see the whole matter.

Diara :- But how can we reach there ?

Duma :- If we have divine suits, there may be other powers activated in it. It's tme to test these.

Lets try first cliff hooks of our gloves and shoes. We all will jump from here and try to stick and climb the rock. Cliff will automatically emerge out and we will anchor on the rocky surface of hill. Let's do.

Diara :- What if hooks will not come out or we will not getting enough anchor grip? We will directly fall into in this unknown hell.

Dodi :- First let me do. We dogs have some natural skills to climb, then you all follow me.

Duma :- Just wait, let me consult with D-Brain.

D-Brain, can you help us to know whether all powers of Divine D suits are fully activated or still not?

D-Brain :- Yes master, as per my sensor's information, all the divine powers of your suits are now fully activated. You can trust these.

Diara :- Will hooks of our shoes and gloves come out automatically if we jump and strike the rocky surface ?

D-Brain :- Sure they will work, but for safer side, you have to adjust your antigravity button accordingly so your body weight. It will be significantly reduced and you can climb the rock easily.

Diara :- Thanks D-Brain. Friends Lets make our debut as a superheroes. Let's go.

They jumped and cliff hooks came out easily. They adjusted their bodyweight by using antigravity power button and sticked to the wall of rock. Then they smoothly started climbing and after few minutes reached near trench.

Dodi :- Boss, my doubt is now reality, these are uranium ores and this is a uranium mine.

Duma :- Oh Jesus! What an exciting, threatening and frightening news is it ? We have uranium mines in our neighbourhood and still we were unaware. Who is stealing this precious metal ? If those two monsters monkeys are doing it, whom they are working for ?

Diara:- I have read in a current affairs science magazine that there are some miscredents who are trying to do nuclear test in some unknown islands of this continent. Their aims are very dangerous. But magazine does not claim whether it is true. If it is true, it's fatal.

Dasmond:- It is possibility that one of such groups might have trained such creatures for their own benefits. We have another reason to worry that our Dictator General Mussava should not know about this information. Its very dangerous to have nuclear mines control in the hands of such a cruel person. He can do anything for his own vetsed interest. We should keep it as secret otherwise one trouble will give rise to many tensions like nuclear fission process.

Duma:- Yes, you are right, we have to catch these demon creatures as soon as possible to get more lead in this mission. Only then we may know about their preparators.

Dasmond :- Yes, but how? We have some powers, but are these enough to overpower them ?

Diara :- We have to find their weaknesses and for it we have to penetrate in their zone.

Duma :- Let's do search operation for a while in nearby area, we may find some more information. Then we will directly go to the city area.

After activation of some divine powers, their work was now becoming relatively much convenient. The scanners of their lenses had some excellent zoom powers so they were seeing the microscopic objects easily. Night vision cameras were also fully working. Sniffing power of Dodi had increased manyfolds. After few moments of extensive search operation, they found something worthy. The scene in the forest was horrible. There was burning heap of dead bodies of monkeys all around. A stinking smell were making breathing more difficult. These were evidences of Dark Monkeys' cruelty. Whole troops of monkeys were dead by now. Their skin is completely burnt. This scene was reminding how deadly the attack was. Only few bones were left. They all shocked to watch this heart wrenching scene.

Duma :- It was the identical attack that they did on us, but surprising we survived and even transformed into more powerful than ever.

Dodi :- Boss, it seems as a minor nuclear attack. Its foul smell indicating that they might have used uranium but in very small amount.

Diara :- Its very panic news. If they are not stopped, They will turn city into ruins very soon. Their intention are clear. They will not spare anyone. We have to search and stop them.

Duma :- It means, if nuclear attack does not affect us, we can definitely stop them. Dont worry. Let's do it.

Dasmond (picking something from ground) :- Just wait, see it what is this. Its an electronic chip like instrument, everything around is burnt but it is safe.

Duma :- What is it ? D- Brain can you identify it ?

D-Brain :- Master, It is an electronic chip which might be fitted in body parts of a living being. It is a memory enhancing chip. It is thermal insensitive means no effect of heat or cold on it. Someone might have used it to enhance its memory.

Duma :- There is definitely someone who is playing the game behind curtain. Let's lift the curtain. Lets keep it with us. It will be helpful later. Now let's move towards city.

In a coordinated way, all switched on the antigravity button of their divine suits and flew in the sky directing towards city where they had to control both the brothers of demolition.

12

The turnmoil in M-4

Mr Mbaka :- Hello Dr Ming, Have you reestblished communication with our soldiers of the mission, Urani and Plutoni ?

Dr Ming :- Yes, I have traced their location, but they are not following our instructions, I suspect we have lost our communication control over them. Their neurocontrol system is either damaged or malfunctioned.

Mr Mbaka :- You mean to say that they are completely out of our control.

Dr Ming :- Yes for now, we can say that. I can still repair it, but it may take time.

Mr MBaka :- How long ?

Dr Ming :- One to two days or more.

Milanikova :- Is their autonomy can affect us ?

Dr Ming :- Not very sure, but there are chances that they may turn hostile and violent. They don't recognise their ultimate bosses or aims and cause aimless destruction. They suddenly start monopoly.

Mr Mbaka :- Their uncontroled behavious is very very threatening for us and our mission.

Milanikova :- Then what to do ?

Mr Mbaka :- In my opinion, we should kill them.

MDC :- We have invested much on them. Is it wise to destroy them ?

Mr Mbaka :- I can understand your concern, but we have no ther option left. If they start destruction and fall in the trap of other organizations or if in any circumstances they opted to surrender themselves, our whole mission will be under scanner.

Milanikova :- I have same opinion, we can recreate dark monkeys, but if they are captured there, our mission will be in danger.

Dr Ming :- You are right, but we have one more option with us. We have their remote control. Blue button of it can diffuse their power to catch them alive and red button can blast them into pieces in case of any failure. Its only option if we can exercise.

Mr Mbaka :- Sergeant, what you have to say ?

Milanikova :- I am ready to operate it. Where is their location right now ?

Dr Ming :- They are about to reach in the south of the Sudalu city.

Milanikova :- I am going to Sudalu city right now in my ultra boat. Give me one bulletproof jacket, one of the most advance machine gun and this remote.

Mr Mbaka :- Are you going alone. Don't you need anyone to assist you ?

Milanikova :- No, I can't do that, its very very secret mission. I can't compromise it. More person in the mission mean more chances of misunderstanding ? If anyone caught, wounded, its not safe. Even if I failed or caught, I will blow myself but never let the mission failed.

Mr Mbaka :- Hats off Sargeant, until warrior like you are a part, the mission will never fail. All the best.

Dr Ming :- Wait, wear this metal band on your wrist.

Milanikova :- How will it work ?

Dr Ming :- It has sensor. Same sensors are planted in the body of Urani and plutoni. When you will reach with in the 1 KM range near them. It will start alarming and you will get their exact location.

Milanikova :- Thats great. Tie it to my wrist.

Dr Ming :- It will also keep tract your location as it is also linked to our master control system.

Milanikova :- Ok. Then good bye for now.

Mr Mbaka :- Good luck sergeant, May you succeed in your mission.

After half an hour of preparation, Sergeant Milanikova left for his final assignment.

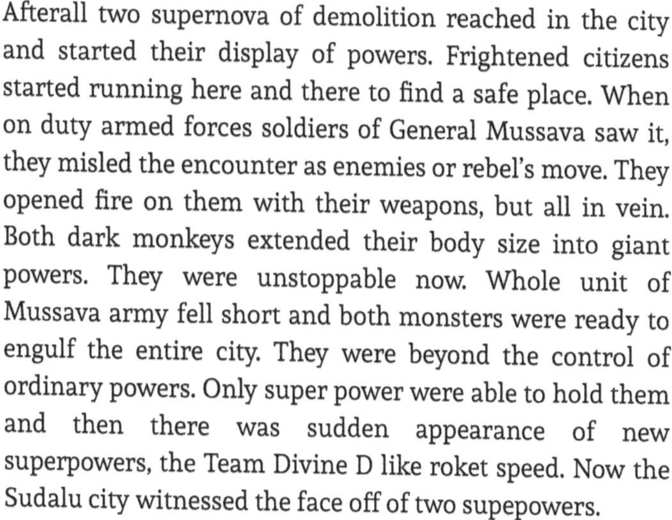

Afterall two supernova of demolition reached in the city and started their display of powers. Frightened citizens started running here and there to find a safe place. When on duty armed forces soldiers of General Mussava saw it, they misled the encounter as enemies or rebel's move. They opened fire on them with their weapons, but all in vein. Both dark monkeys extended their body size into giant powers. They were unstoppable now. Whole unit of Mussava army fell short and both monsters were ready to engulf the entire city. They were beyond the control of ordinary powers. Only super power were able to hold them and then there was sudden appearance of new superpowers, the Team Divine D like roket speed. Now the Sudalu city witnessed the face off of two supepowers.

Duma :- Hey giant dark monkeys. Just stop. You need to go back. We will save our beloved Sudalu city.

Urani :- Hahaha, you little rats, are you still alive ? How? But not this time. You have chosen the messenger of death. Now none can save you.

Dasmond :- See, we are not your enemy. Someone has hacked your mind. You surrender peacefully. We will not harm you.

Plutoni (furiously) :- You will not harm us ? You daydreamers, we will harm you to such an extent that your existence will be wiped out.

Urani :- We will burn you to ashes. None has hacked our mind. We are new rulers of this universe. We will rule the world.

By saying this, he suddenly attacked with his nuclear power to Duma and Dasmond, but instead of burning, they both became stronger.

Urani :- Oh no, whats happening here, it is impossible. Why my attack is not working ?

Duma :- It will not work. That's why we are saying ? Just surrender yourself. You will be spared.

Plutoni :- Do you think we are fools ? You are just playing tricks. Now face my next gift attack.

He attacked on bystanders Diara and Dodi, the result was same. Infuriated Plutoni just used his steel fingers like weapon coming out from his hands and held throat of Dasmond with tight grip. Seeing it, Duma tried to save his friend but mighty Plutoni threw him away.

Duma (writhing in pain) :- Ouch, what a power. He had almost broken my backbone. We alltogather can't overpower even single of them.

Dodi :- Boss hope you are safe, ask D-Brain for help now.

Duma :- Oh yes, I forgot. D-Brain can you suggest how to tackle these monsters

D-Brain :- Master you can't overpower them with use of muscle power, they are power packed with nuclear enerygy. Just use trick, use your cadmium rod gun. Then their nuclear reaction will be slow down and their power will be drained. This is only way to tackle nuclear power.

Duma picked up gun and stood up with agility of a tiger as his name reflects (Swahili language meaning) and opend fire cadmium bullets at Urani. He felt a shock like electric current and fell on ground. Plutoni also surprised to see and suddenly Dasmond managed to escape his tight grip.

The battle of Sudalu

Urani :- Oh God whats happening to me, something draining energy from my body. Aah

Plutoni :- Don't worry brother, I will teach them a lesson.

Urani :- AAh, No bro, it's time to learn a lesson, not to teach them. Take me to a safer place. They have this super gun which is reducing our power. Let's go to a safer place and recharge again. Come on, run.

Plutoni:- Ok Brother as you wish.

Instantly he shoulder lifted Urani and jumped towards sea beach.

Diara :- Hey friends ! They are running. Let's catch them alive.

Dasmond : Follow them

Suddenly Plutoni threw a balloon like object on them which exploded. There was diffusion of a poisonous gas all around. All Divine D members were temporarily blind for few minutes. When they regained their eyesights, both giants were disappeared.

Dasmond :- What was it ? I was nearly blind for few minutes.

Dodi :- As per my sniffing scale, this gas was a new invention from chemical pioneers. These masks have saved us otheriswise it was a deadly gas experiment.

Duma :- D- Brain Can you please tell in which direction they fled?

D-Brain :- Master as per my signals, they went toward sea shore. One of them is appearing hurted and other shoulder lifted him.

Duma :- Thanks. So friends let's catch them alive before it is too late. Our cadmium rod is working well against them. This is the golden chance to grab them.

Diara :- Now it is confirmed that they are made up of nuclear power. It's a dangerous game now. Let's grab them alive.

Then Team Divine D flew in the sky for their destination.

14
The End of unruly nuclear powers

After some time, Plutoni reached at sea shore along with Urani on his shoulders

Plutoni (putting Urani on ground):- Hello Bro how are you feeling now ?

Urani :- Slightly better but it seems someone has halved my energy level.

Plutoni :- Don't know who is this young team and how they got so much power in few hours ? Our attack moves are not affecting them anymore.

Urani :- I also don't know, but I can't fight for longer. I need more nuclear power.

Plutoni :- We need to hide ourselves for sometime. We should wait for sometime.

Urani :- Take me to the jungle quickly.

Plutoni :- Let me take a chance. I will try to transmit my energy to certain level.

He put the chip (planted in his thumb) on Urani's forehead to transfer the nuclear power as his bosses instructed him in the training. After doing so for sometime....

Urani :- Now I feel much better. It seems my energy is back, Now I can fight for sometime.

Plutoni :- Let Not engage with this young team, if they attack with their strange gun, we are not in a position to defend ourselves.

Urani :- Now lets fled to the jungle.

Then suddenly a zoom sound attracted their attention and before they looked back, team Divine D landed in front of them.

Duma :- Hello guys, we are here again. What a surprise get together. We traced you location again.

Then brother of destruction took their attack position again.

Plutoni :- Don't underestimate us. Let us go. We don't want to confront you.

Duma :- Listen, it's a big conspiracy. They are using you both. Don't be a part of it. Let us expose them.

Urani :- Give us a safer way or get ready for final face off.

As Duma aimed at Plutoni he resized himself to tiny shape with a click of button and jumped into the sea and Urani also followed him and disappeared into the water.

Duma :- Oh God! what a magic. D-Brain what to do now?

D-Brain :- Master, you have the power to walk on the water or swim in the water. Just adjust your antigravity power and follow them. Hurry up before they will go beyond my range.

First hesitating, then they keep their steps on water and walked slowly on it. Then they gained confidence and started running like an athlete. It was thrilling experience for all of them. They followed the direction of supernovas of destruction and soon approached them which were still facing difficulty in swimming. Then they instantly resized themselves as giant again.

Duma :- Hey Hey Hey, Dont be naughty. We will follow you everywhere.

Plutoni :- I don't understand why are you following us? Spare us. We will never come back again.

Dasmond :- Who will repair the damage you already caused? People behind you are having ill itnention. They are aiming to control all humanity and universe. Try to understand. They are not good people. Please help to trace them.

Urani :- Which people ? We don't even remember. What are you talking about ?

Diara :- Come with us. We promise, you will be safe

Urani :- You can't block us. Stay away.

By warning them, Plutoni suddenly attacked Diara with his metallic blade like fingers but this time Dasmond was also prepared in advance. He quickly aimed his supergun, clicked second button of it and fired a spray of a huge quantity of sticky glue like substance which trapped Plutoni and he was unable to move. That glue freezed him like a statue. Dodi also sprinkled a ink like liquid into the eyes of Urani from his paw. It barred his eyesight completely. Diara also took advantage of the situation and an thick metallic chain emerged out with just a click from her hand. It was just an unsure bid which worked nicely. She tied both urani and plutoni with it. The material of the chain was not ordinary one, so both supermonkey couldn't managed to break it. All the plan was working well for team Divine D before a unusual thing happed there.

Suddenly a giant shark like object appeared from sea, pushed away team Divine D and both giant dark monkeys. During this momentary act, metallic chain was broken and both were free. Before the Divine D warriors could get up and understand what has happened, there were two big bang explosion blasting and claimning both lives of Urani and Plutoni's. Their bodies were torn and tatters into pieces. None could understand it. Mysterious giant shark like fish also disappeared in the blue depth of sea water.

The end of unruly nuclear powers

Duma :- Friends, are you all ok?

All others in a single voice : Yes we are all right. But how a giant fish did this suddenly ?

Duma :- I am also shocked. Alas! We couldn't catch them alive.

Diara :- Don't worry we have not failed completely. We have achieved a lot.

Dasmond :- We are blessed with these superpowers. Now onwards, we are a team of young African superheroes, THE TEAM DIVINE D.

Dodi :- Lets search some more evidences from their mortal remains scattered here in pieces. We may get some clues. We have to trace the preparators of this dangerous nuclear power game.

Then they dived into the sea water and collected some evidences which may help them to take lead the mission in near future. Then they sang Divine D anthem.

Onething they didn't notice were many people already gathered on the sea shore watching them. Few kids exclaimed with joy after watching the team of new young superheroes. They yelled " Now the bad powers are finished, see our own team of young superheroes is here to save us. People who have doubt that African soil can't produce their own superheoes, should come and see the **TEAM OF OUR OWN YOUNG SUPERHEROES.**

Team Divine D now again moved for their new mission.

Mystery Still Stands

But still there are few unsolved mysterious questions in their mind and in our's also. Afterall who killed Urani and Plutoni and why ? Is it that mysterious giant shark fish like object or anyone else ? Did Sargeant Milanikova and M-4 succeeded in their mision? How did a shark like fish gather immense power to kill supergiants dark monkeys in just a moment? Until knowing answers this mystery, team Divine D will not sit quietly. What will be their next mission ?

Readers will get answers of these unsolved questions very soon in next part of Divine D Series

Thanks for reading

www.ingramcontent.com/pod-product-compliance
Lightning Source LLC
Chambersburg PA
CBHW020457160726
47991CB00007B/2698